FOR

EVAN, TEGAN

AND POPPY

EP LOCKED

5000 pieces

MONKEY P

zle

5000 pieces

150 PIECES

First published in
Great Britain in 2008
by Egmont UK Limited
239 Kensington High Street
London W8 6SA

Text copyright © Jim Helmore 2008
Illustrations copyright © Karen Wall 2008
The author and illustrator have
asserted their moral rights
A CIP catalogue for this title is
available from The British Library

ISBN - 978 1 4052 4200 4 (Hardback)
ISBN - 978 1 4052 4201 1 (Paperback)
All rights reserved
10 9 8 7 6 5 4 3 2 1
Printed in Singapore

LOOK OUT,
STRIPY HORSE!

Jim Helmore and Karen Wall

EGMONT

Magic was at work in the stripy horse's shop.

Magic . . . and mischief!

Nothing
looked
quite
the way
it should.

"Help!" barked Hermann, the draught excluder. "I've been tied in a knot!"

"Goodness!" twittered Muriel from her lampshade. "I've been scribbled on!"

"ATISHOO!" sneezed Roly, the saltpot penguin. "I've been filled with pepper."

"And I've been been filled with salt," groaned his pepperpot partner, Pitch.

"Oh dear, oh dear!"
Mortice, the lion-shaped lock,
looked out from his wooden trunk.
"Someone forgot to lock me up
and now the monkeys have escaped!"

"Monkeys?" asked
the stripy horse.

DANGER!
JIGSAW PUZZLES

KEEP LOCKED

"Those **mischievous** monkeys from the monkey puzzle!" growled the lion. "And they've taken my key! What **shall** I do without it?"

"Try this . . ." said Hermann popping a pencil into Mortice's mouth.

DANGER! JIGSAW PUZZLES

"**Mmmmm,**" chomped the lion.

"Look out, stripy horse!" flapped Muriel.

A monkey darted from the shadows and ran straight towards them.

W H E E E E

"Not so fast, you pesky primate!"
cried Roly and Pitch.

eeee!

"There goes my key!"
roared Mortice.

But the monkey
slipped out
of their net.

"Stop thief!" bellowed Hermann,
as the mischievous monkey swung up and away.

"Oh, they're slippery, those
monkeys," sighed the lion.

"Don't worry,"
said the stripy horse.
"I'm very good with
slippery objects!"

And he galloped after Hermann.

CRASH!

They were all so busy watching the monkey that they forgot to watch one another!

PLONK!

THUD!

WALLOP!

"Well, you won't catch a monkey like that," said Mortice.

"How **are** we supposed to catch them?" asked the stripy horse.

"We must get all the monkeys to stand on top of the jigsaw," explained Mortice. "Then shout, 'ELZZUP YEKNOM' as loudly as we can and the monkeys will be pulled back into the puzzle."

"ELZZUP YEKNOM?" said Hermann. "That sounds like fun!"

"But we'll need to make the jigsaw first," said Pitch. "Come on, Roly!"

"I've had an idea,"
trilled Muriel as
the final pieces
slotted together.
"Follow me everyone . . ."

They all squeezed under the sideboard.

"To get the monkeys back on top of their puzzle," whispered Muriel,

"we'll need something they can't resist."

"What do you mean?" asked Pitch.

"BANANAS!" woofed Hermann.

"Exactly!" said Muriel. "We'll give the monkeys
the biggest banana they've ever seen."
"And where do we get one of those?" asked the stripy horse.
Muriel smiled. "Wait and see!"

"What do you think, everyone?" chuckled Hermann.

"Are you **sure** this
is going to work?"
grumbled Mortice.

The friends crawled back under the sideboard and waited. All was silent except for the ticking of the cuckoo clock.

Then a shadow darted across the room.

Slowly, slowly one of the monkeys stole into view . . . then another,

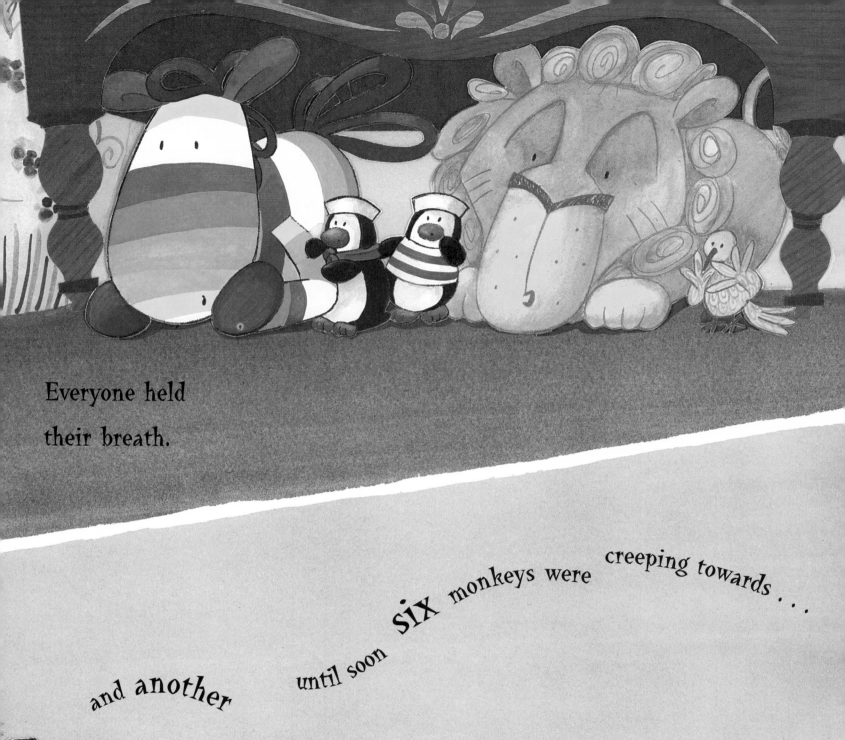

Everyone held
their breath.

and another   until soon six monkeys were   creeping towards . . .

...Hermann the prize banana!

"EL..."
began Roly.

"Wait!" hushed Muriel.
"Don't shout
until they're **all**
on top of the puzzle."

The monkeys crept closer.

"**Now!**" whispered the stripy horse.

"ELZZUP YEKNOM!"

everyone cried.

FLASH!

BANG!

WHIZZ!

The shop lit up
with sparkling,
crackling light.

The monkeys were tossed
into the air,
and then,
with a great **WHOOSH**
they were sucked
back down into
the puzzle.

"Quickly!" said Muriel. "Put the puzzle back inside the trunk before those monkeys get up to any more tricks."

"But we can't lock
the puzzle away
until I get my key back,"
said Mortice.
"Where can it be?"

"CUCKOO!"

It was

five o'clock.

The cuckoo at the top of the clock

shot in and out, five noisy times.

"There it is!"

flapped Muriel.

The lion's missing key

dropped from

the cuckoo's beak.

"Look **out below!**" called Muriel.

"**Got you!**" said the stripy horse as he caught the shiny key.

Click!

The stripy horse turned the key
in the lion's mouth
and the monkey puzzle
was safely locked away.

"Mmmmm," chomped Mortice.
"Thank you, stripy horse. Pencils
are all well and good, but you
can't beat a nice tasty key."

DANGER!
JIGSAW PUZZLES

KEEP LOCKED

Day was breaking as the
friends settled back
into their places
for a well-earned rest.

And all was quiet in the shop once more . . .